THE AMAZING VOYAGE OF JACKIE GRACE

by Matt Faulkner

SCHOLASTIC HARDCOVER

SCHOLASTIC INC.

New York

Created with love for Amy

Library of Congress Cataloging-in-Publication Data
Faulkner, Matt.
The amazing voyage of Jackie Grace.
Summary: A young boy's imagination takes him on a
wonderful adventure.
[1. Imagination – Fiction] I. Title.
PZ7.F2765Am 1987   [E]   86-31485
ISBN 0-590-40713-9

12 11 10 9 8 7 6 5 4 3 2   7 8 9/8 0 1 2/9
Printed in the U.S.A.   23

FIRST SCHOLASTIC PRINTING, AUGUST 1987

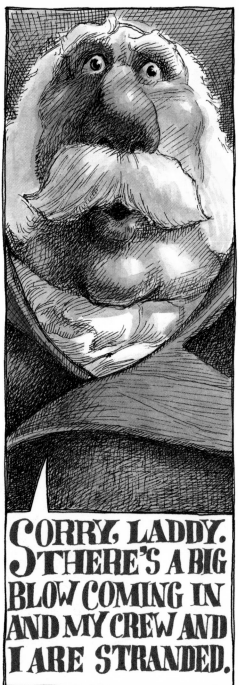

Here's my crew now!

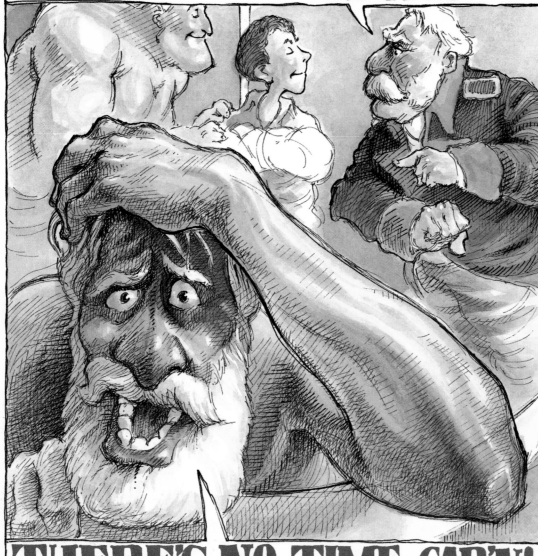

RIG UP A SAIL!

IT WON'T BE LONG NOW, LADDY! WE'LL HAVE THOSE PIRATES RIGHT WHERE WE WANT THEM!
PIRATES?

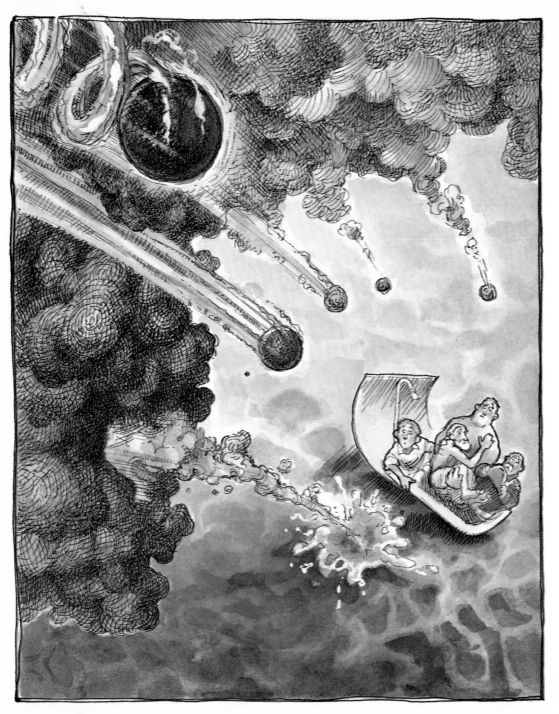

FIRE AT WILL!

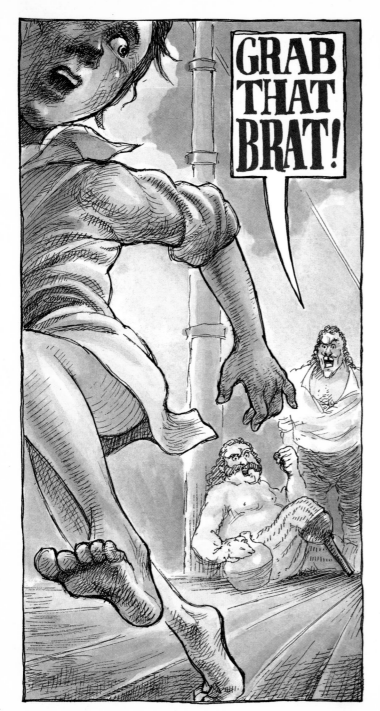

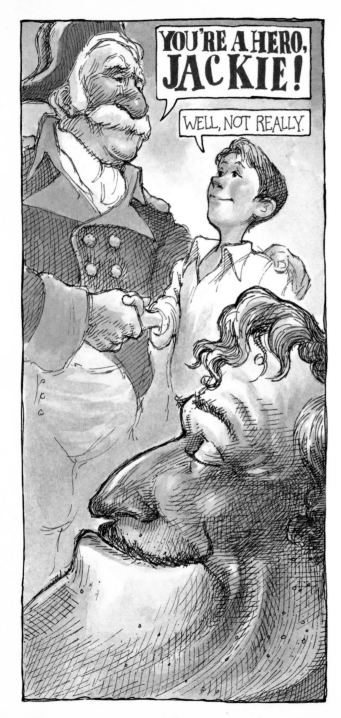

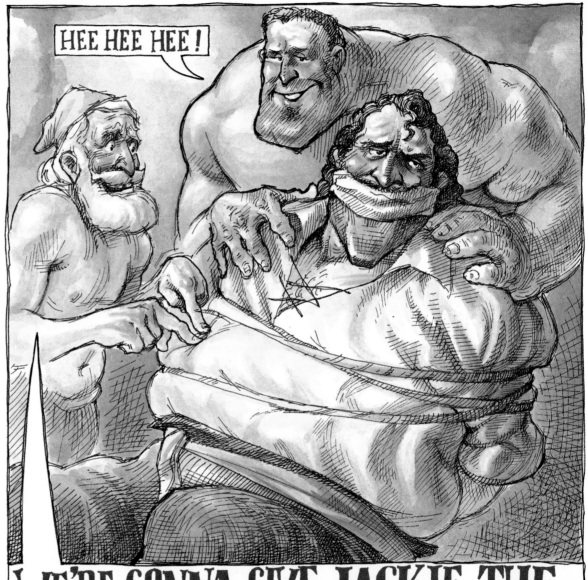